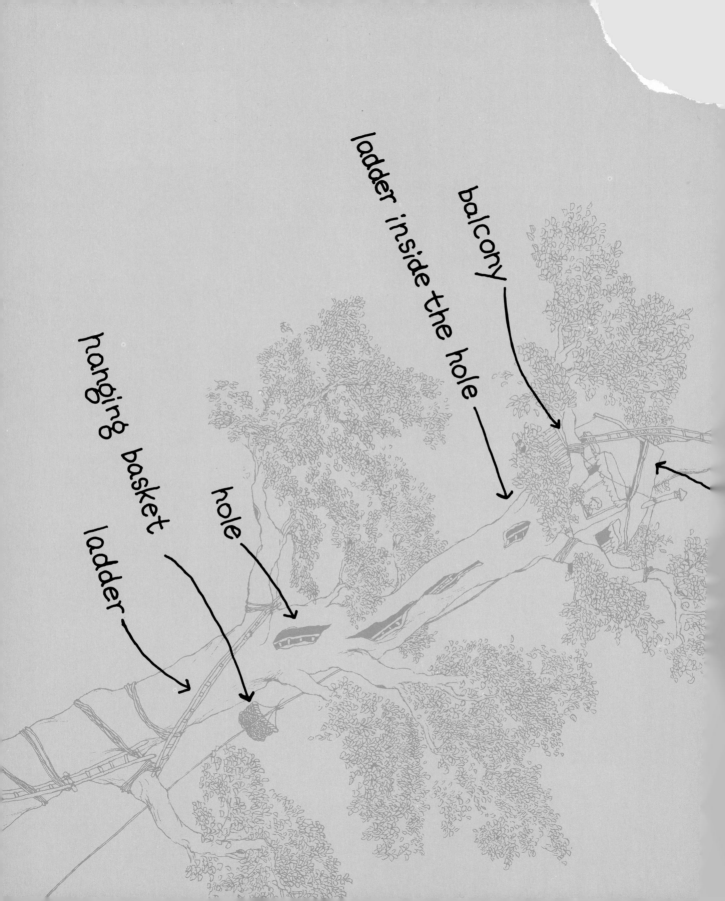

balcony

ladder inside the hole

hanging basket

hole

ladder

jays }
chickadees } live here

lookout
platform

ladder

ladder

squirrels' house

ladder

Kaoru's tree house

ENGLISH TEXT BY
HITOMI JITODAI AND CAROL EISMAN

First U.S. Edition published in 1989
1   2   3   4   5   6   7   8   9   10

Library of Congress Cataloging in Publication Data
Sato, Satoru, date [Ōkina ki ga hoshii. English] I wish I had a big, big tree / written by
Satoru Sato; illustrated by Tsutomu Murakami; [English text by Hitomi Jitodai &
Carol Eisman].   p.   cm. Translation of: Ōkina ki ga hoshii. Summary: Kaoru
imagines what he would do if he had a big, big tree, where he could build himself a house
and visit the squirrels and birds. ISBN 0-688-07303-4 ISBN 0-688-07304-2 (lib. bdg.)
[1. Trees—Fiction.   2. Imagination—Fiction.]   I. Murakami, Tsutomu, 1943-   ill.
II. Title.
PZ7.S2492Iaaw 1989 [Fic]—dc19   88-8080 CIP AC

I Wish I Had a Big, Big Tree

By Satoru Sato   Illustrated by Tsutomu Murakami

Lothrop, Lee & Shepard Books / New York

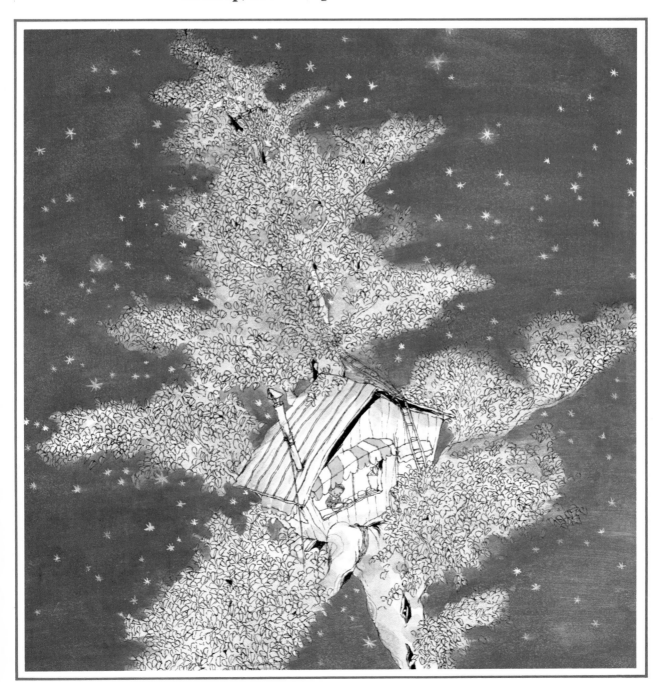

"I wish I had a big, big tree," Kaoru said to his mother, looking out the kitchen window.

"A big tree?" said his mother. She was in the yard, hanging out the clothes to dry. It was a beautiful day.

"Wouldn't you like to climb a big, high tree, Mommy?" Kaoru asked.

"Yes," she said, "but it might be dangerous."

"Oh, no, it wouldn't," Kaoru told her. "I've figured it all out so it wouldn't be dangerous at all."

Kaoru's mother had climbed a tree when she was a little girl. It was not a big tree, but she could still remember how happy she felt.

"It would be fun if we had a tree big enough to climb," she said. She looked around, but in their small, narrow yard there were only three little bushes—two azaleas and one rose—that were no good at all for climbing.

"Yes," said Kaoru. "I wish I had a big tree." He sighed, imagining what he would do with his wonderful tree.

And suddenly he could see the big tree in front of him....

Kaoru's tree is so big and fat that he can't put his arms around the trunk. Even if his father and his mother and his sister, Kayo, held hands, they would barely make a big enough circle to go around it.

Without a ladder he cannot even begin to climb the tree.

"I must have a ladder," Kaoru said to himself.

First he leans the ladder against the lowest branch. Then he ties it very tightly to the tree trunk, so it won't shake.

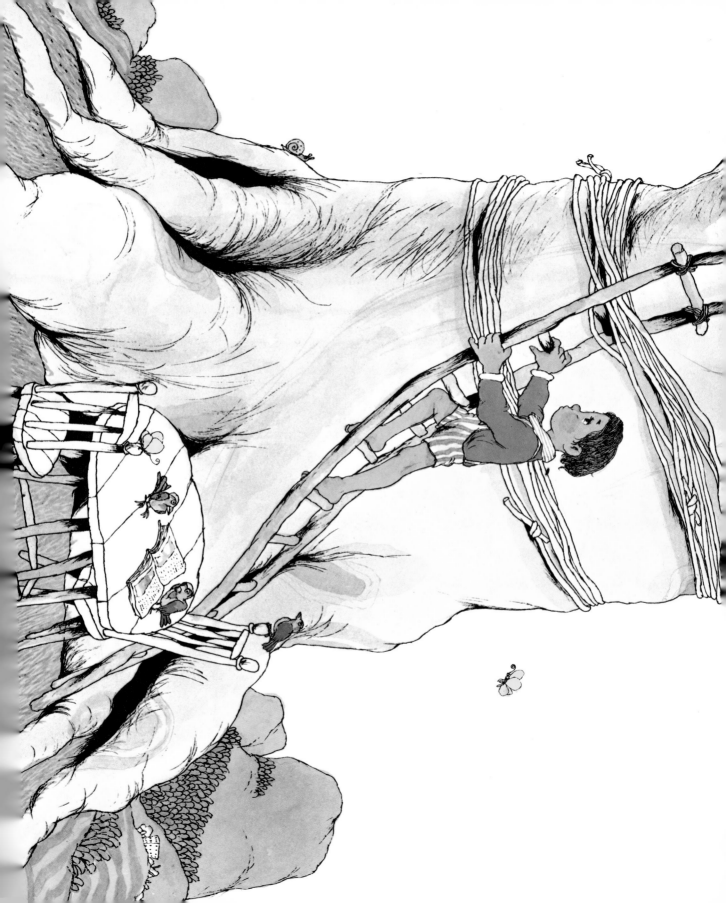

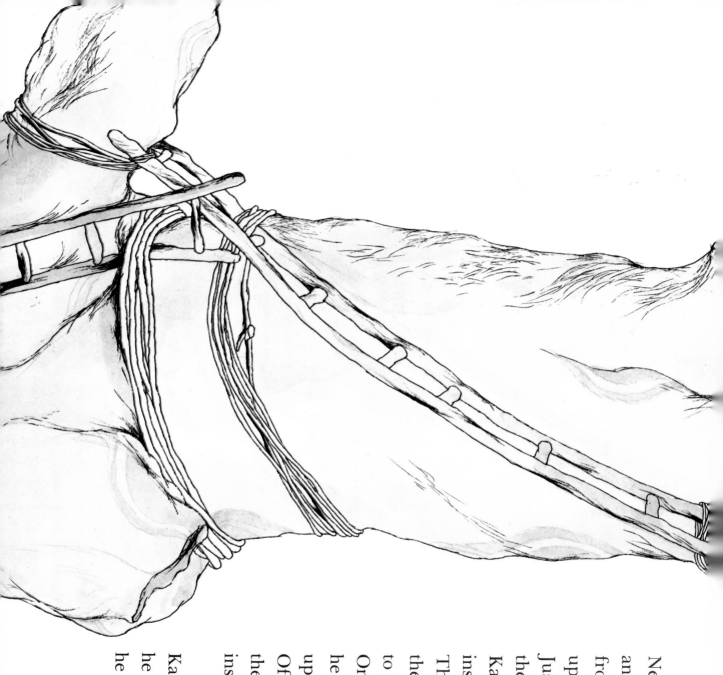

Next, Kaoru has to lean
another short ladder
from the first branch
up to the second.
Just above this branch,
there's a hole in the tree.
Kaoru can see deep
inside the trunk.
The hole is just
the right size for him
to squeeze through.
Once he's inside,
he can climb
up and up and up.
Of course,
there is a ladder
inside the hole.

Kaoru was so excited,
he felt as if
he were really climbing.

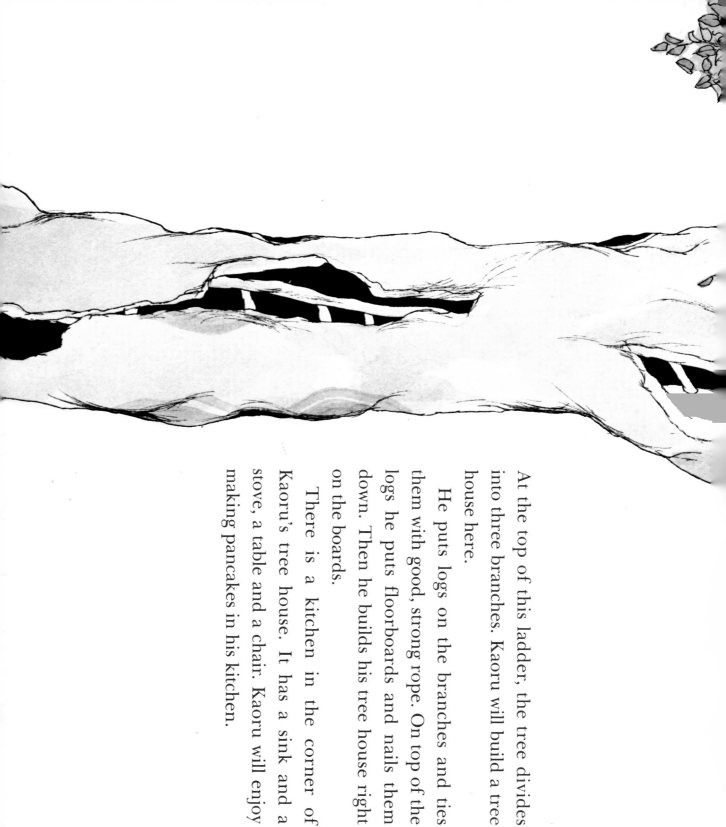

At the top of this ladder, the tree divides into three branches. Kaoru will build a tree house here.

He puts logs on the branches and ties them with good, strong rope. On top of the logs he puts floorboards and nails them down. Then he builds his tree house right on the boards.

There is a kitchen in the corner of Kaoru's tree house. It has a sink and a stove, a table and a chair. Kaoru will enjoy making pancakes in his kitchen.

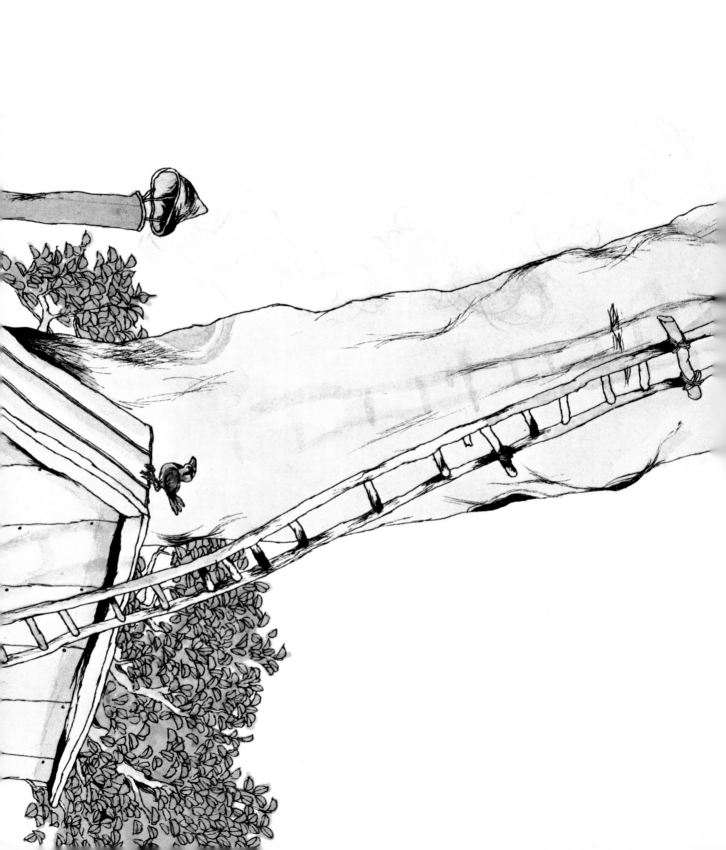

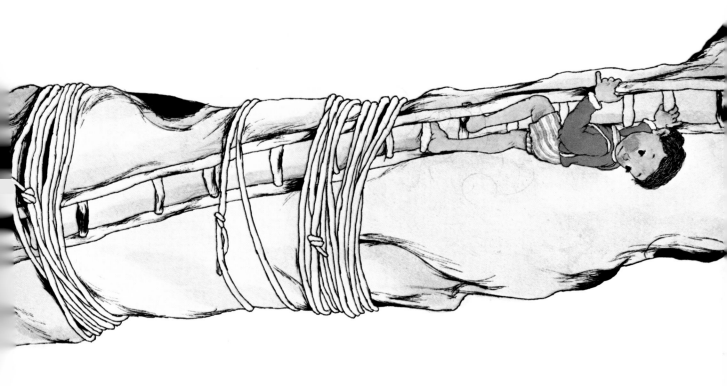

If Kaoru isn't careful,
the pancakes might burn.
Then there would be smoke.
That's why his tree house
has a chimney.

"Should I bring Kayo?"
Kaoru wonders.
His sister is only
three years old,
so she might not be able
to climb the ladder.

"I'll make a hanging basket,
sort of like a swing,
for her," he decides.
It works very easily.
To pull her up,
all Kaoru has to do
is turn the handle.

Outside the tree house,
another ladder takes him
even higher.

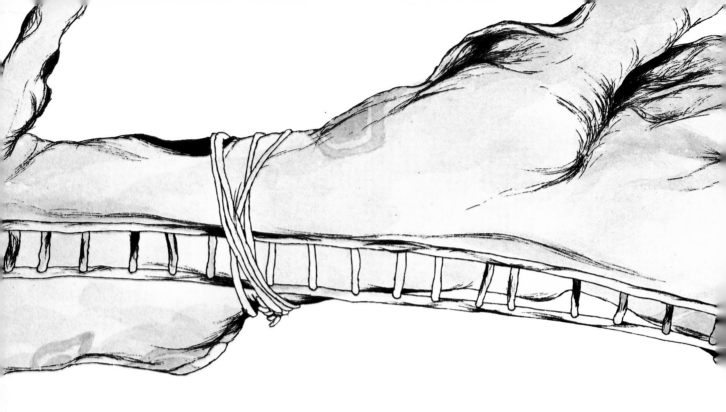

Where a higher branch joins the trunk, there is a small hole. The squirrel and his family live here.

"Hello," Kaoru calls.

The squirrels always hurry out when they hear Kaoru's voice. "Good afternoon, Kaoru," they say politely. After all, Kaoru is the owner of this tree.

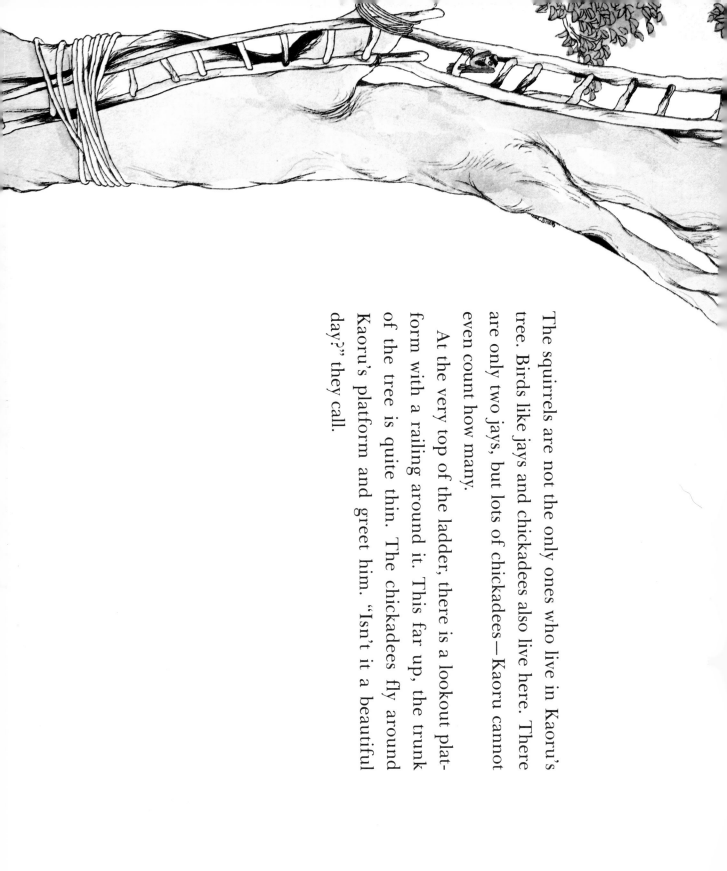

The squirrels are not the only ones who live in Kaoru's tree. Birds like jays and chickadees also live here. There are only two jays, but lots of chickadees—Kaoru cannot even count how many.

At the very top of the ladder, there is a lookout platform with a railing around it. This far up, the trunk of the tree is quite thin. The chickadees fly around Kaoru's platform and greet him. "Isn't it a beautiful day?" they call.

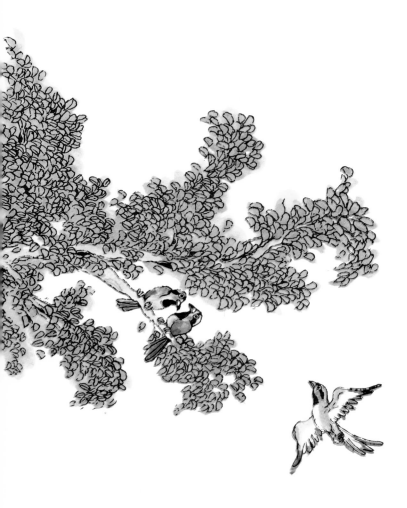

From his lookout platform Kaoru can see the houses in town. The cars look as tiny as beetles. He can also see the faraway mountains. He can see such a great distance because now he is almost at the top of the big tree.

The breeze suddenly comes up and blows his hair. The leaves rustle. The tree is so tall that sometimes it sways a bit in the wind, but Kaoru is not afraid. As long as he holds on tightly, he is completely safe.

"I feel like I can fly!" Kaoru shouts.

"Whee!" Kaoru shouted out loud. "Mommy, I want to tell you about my big tree!"

But Kaoru's mother had finished hanging out the clothes, and Kayo was just waking up from her nap. "Kaoru, not right now, I'm busy," said his mother, hurrying back into the house. "Tell me your story later."

Oh, well, he'd just have to wait. Kaoru went out to the yard and looked up at the sky. Big white clouds, like cotton, were drifting by. It would be summer pretty soon.

Kaoru thought, "When summer comes..."

In the summer,
Kaoru's house
in the big tree
stays cool.
Sometimes
crickets sing
in the house.
Dragonflies
come to visit.
Kaoru is glad
to see them.

After summer, it's autumn.
Kaoru's tree has leaves
all year round, but the leaves
of the other trees turn yellow
and fall to the ground.
Maple and gingko leaves
come flying into the tree house.
The jays and chickadees
help Kaoru sweep them up.
Jays have a habit of collecting
all sorts of unusual things,
and if Kaoru has dropped
any beads, pencils, or buttons,
they might take them away.

Winter.
A cold north wind.
It's snowing hard.
On snowy days
Kaoru and Kayo
light the stove
in the tree house.
When they see smoke
curling out of the chimney,
the squirrels
drop by for a visit
and bring Kaoru walnuts.

Soon spring will come again.
What kind of flowers
will bloom on Kaoru's tree?
Even Kaoru doesn't know.
What color will they be?
Wouldn't it be lovely
if every kind of flower
bloomed at the same time?
They would smell beautiful.
The squirrels, jays, and chickadees
would all be happy.

"I wish I had a big tree like that," said Kaoru. "But I know what—I can draw a picture of it!"

When Kaoru's father came home, Kaoru showed him the picture of the wonderful tree. "See, Daddy," he explained, "you climb this ladder, and then you climb another ladder. Then you come to the place where you get inside the tree trunk. Then you climb the ladder inside the tree, and that brings you to my house."

"That's very interesting," said his father. "You know, I had the same idea a long time ago."

"Did you?" Kaoru was filled with excitement. "Did you really have a big tree like this?"

"No, it's a pity, but I didn't."

"Daddy," Kaoru said, "let's plant a tree that will grow really big. When it gets big enough, we can build a tree house in it together."

"That's a very good idea," his father answered with a smile.

On Sunday, Kaoru and his father planted a tree. Some-day it will grow to an enormous size. But right now, it is smaller than Kaoru.

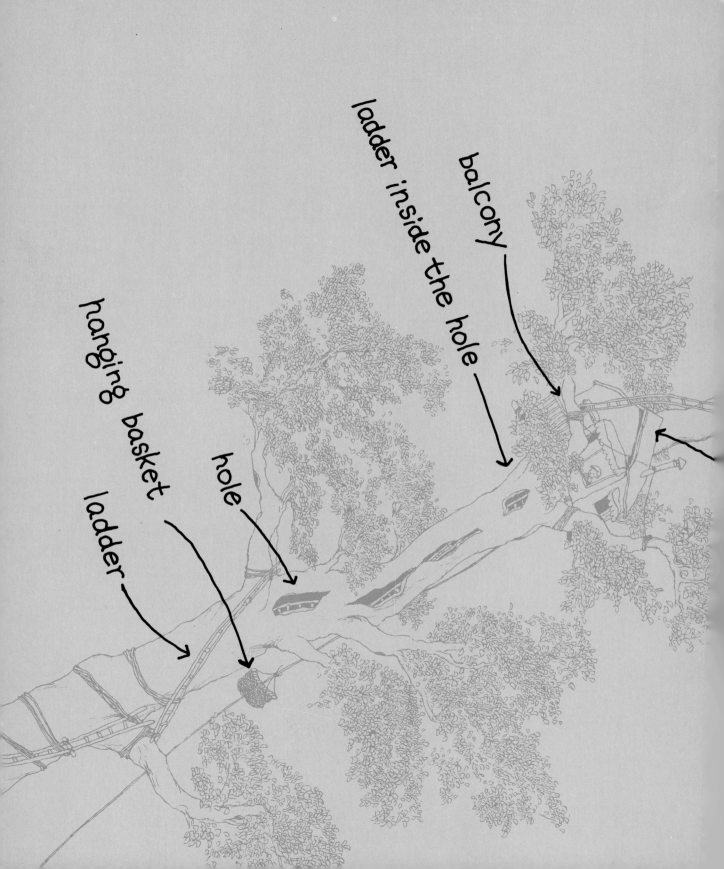

ladder inside the hole

balcony

hanging basket

hole

ladder

jays } live here
chickadees

squirrels' house

ladder

lookout platform

ladder

Kaoru's tree house